THIS WALKER BOOK BELONGS TO:

_____

_____

_____

_____

for Lucy — J. K.
with love for
   Mum and Dad — M. S.

First published 2000 by Walker Books Ltd
87 Vauxhall Walk, London SE11 5HJ

This edition published 2001

10 9 8 7 6 5 4 3 2 1

Text © 2000 Jenny Koralek
Illustrations © 2000 Mandy Sutcliffe

The right of Jenny Koralek to be identified
as author of this work has been asserted by
her in accordance with the Copyright, Designs
and Patents Act 1988

This book has been typeset in Usherwood Medium

Printed in Hong Kong

British Library Cataloguing in Publication Data:
a catalogue record for this book is
available from the British Library

ISBN 0-7445-8229-6

Night Ride to Nanna's

JENNY KORALEK

ILLUSTRATED BY

MANDY SUTCLIFFE

WALKER BOOKS
AND SUBSIDIARIES
LONDON · BOSTON · SYDNEY

*Amy loves the night ride
to Nanna's.*

*She loves the night ride and
the way it begins...*

When Mum says, "We'll have
supper on the early side and just
a quick wash instead of a bath."
And Amy puts on her pyjamas
and her soft red slippers
and Mum gathers up baby Sam.

*Amy loves the night ride
to Nanna's.*

Dad turns out the lights
and locks the front door,
and the house goes dark
and the house goes quiet.

"Goodnight, house!"
Amy calls.
"I'll be back soon!"

At first Dad goes so slowly
because it's the rush hour
and everybody's going somewhere.

Mum and Dad sing
My Old Man Said Follow the Van,
and Sam drops his bottle on the floor
and chatters on until he falls asleep.

Amy sits back and looks and looks
at everything.

Here comes the market.

Amy smells its smells
through the window
open at the top.

She sees the fire glowing out
of holes where chestnuts are
roasting, a cat on the pavement,
oranges and lemons piled up
high, Nanna's favourite flowers
standing blue and yellow
in buckets in a row ...

and a lucky boy
holding a big red balloon.

Tired grown-ups look down from a bus.

Sometimes they smile

and Amy smiles and waves.

Sometimes children make faces

and she makes faces back.

And then comes the bridge with all its little lights!

The lights are in the water too, as if the river were full of sparklers.

Amy loves the night ride

to Nanna's house.

Dad goes faster and faster

and Amy is not sure where they are.

She sees black shapes against the sky,

huge dark buildings like giants sleeping,

and the tall clock tower. And Mum says,

"It's past seven o'clock

and look who's not in bed!"

Then they come to the park
and Amy sees the path
all white in the night
going up to the hill where
she knows tomorrow morning
Grandpa will let her help him
fly his kite.

They're nearly there
and Dad slows down.

"I know this corner!" says Amy.

"I know this road! I know this house!"

It's all lit up and Nanna's at the window.

Grandpa's at the door.

"Hello, Night Rider,"

says Grandpa.

"Let me give you

a helping hand."

They go up the steps

into the house

to Nanna in the hall.

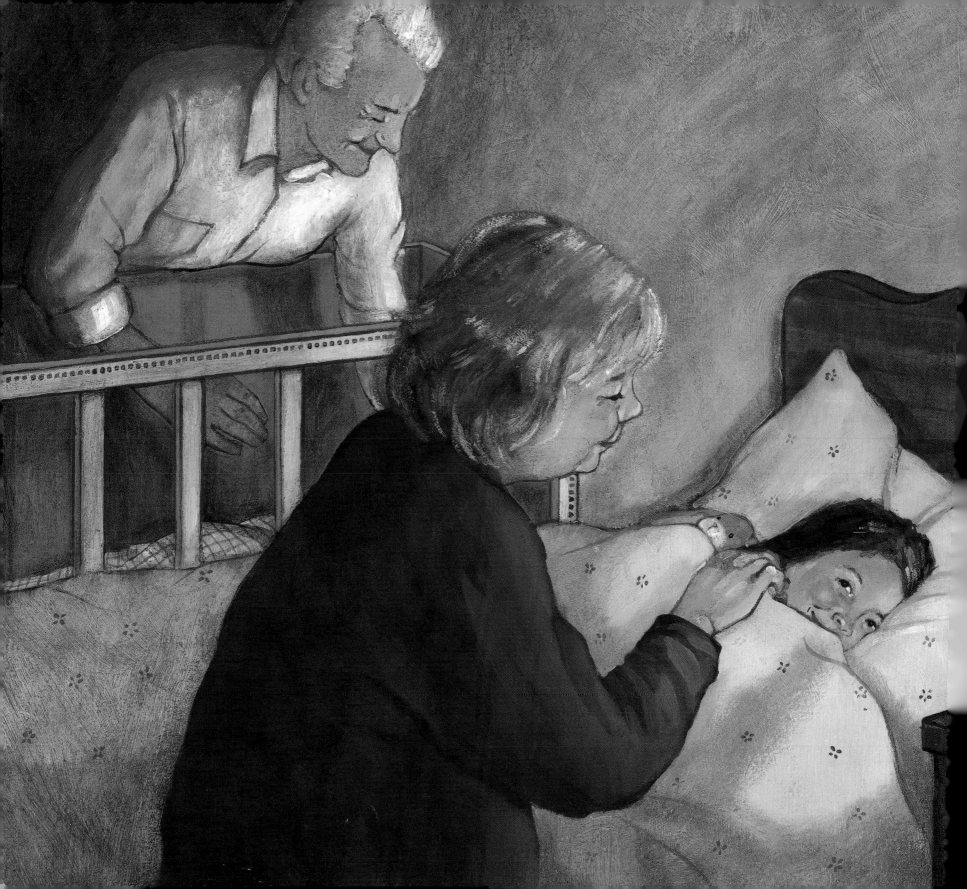

*Amy loves the night ride
to Nanna's house.*

She loves the way it ends...

When Nanna has tucked her
into the bed that's always
ready for her...

When she's kissed Mum and
Dad and Grandpa and Nanna
and they've all kissed her...

When she's ready to fall asleep
but before she does, she hears

everyone laughing at one of Dad's jokes ...

their voices coming softly
through the open door.

Jenny Koralek says her inspiration for **Night Ride to Nanna's** came to her when "my two small grandchildren came to stay with us, having travelled across the city and the river in the night to our house. I believe every child in the world is entitled to such an experience – to travel from one safe, known, loved place to another."

Jenny Koralek is the author of sixteen books for children, including the Walker picture book *The Boy and the Cloth of Dreams*. Born in South Africa and educated in England and France, Jenny now lives in London.

Mandy Sutcliffe says of her illustrations for *Night Ride to Nanna's*, "I wanted my paintings to convey the warmth the words hold for me. As I worked, I remembered childhood journeys – the cosy feeling of sitting in the back seat of the car, watching the world go by."

Mandy Sutcliffe was born in Manchester and studied Illustration at Leeds Metropolitan University. During a three-month stay in Paris she began studying and painting pictures of children, and her fascination with their easy yet animated gestures is evident in *Night Ride to Nanna's*, which is Mandy's first picture book.